VAMPIRE BABY

Kelly Bennett

ILLUSTRATED BY Paul Meisel

CANDLEWICK PRESS

This is my sister, Tootie.
Tootie used to be a cuddly, ga-ga-goo-goo,
I-want-my-ba-ba baby.

Then, one night, she turned into . . .

VAMPIRE BABY!

It happened when Tootie got teeth—*two* in *one* night.
They were not teensy-weensy, itsy-bitsy baby teeth, either.
They were long, sharp, pointed FANGS.

"Canines," the doctor said. "Most unusual."
We should have known right then.

Tootie sinks her fangs into everything:

the furniture,

my catcher's mitt,

my toys,

my bike tires,

my superhero
action figures . . .

and especially *me.*

"YOUCH, TOOTIE! NO BITE!"

Nothing is safe from Vampire Baby.
You'd think I could just keep away from her.

But it's not that easy.
Tootie starts acting extra smiley and adorable.

She gurgles and waves her chubby baby arms, begging me to hold her.

She waits until I'm within fang range, and then . . .

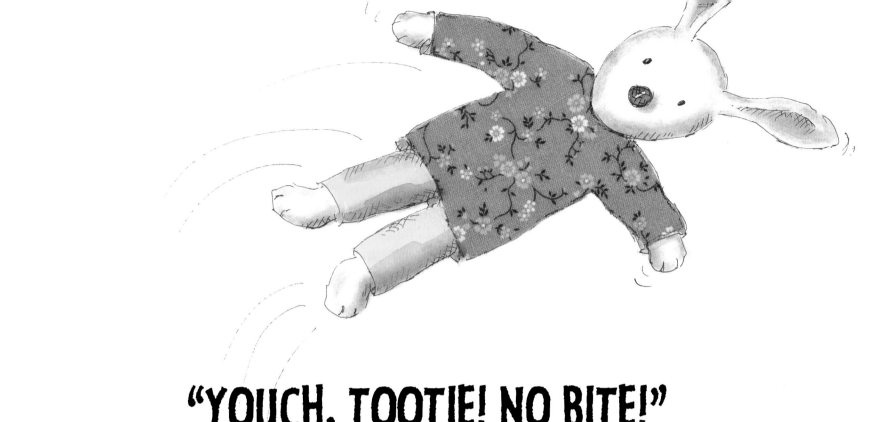

"YOUCH, TOOTIE! NO BITE!"

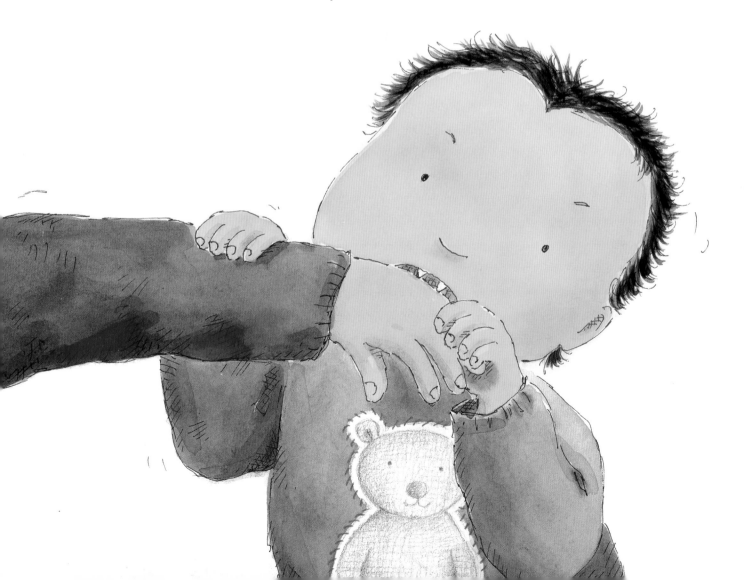

I had to convince Mom and Dad that Tootie really was a vampire baby.
"Your sister is not a vampire," Mom said. "Biting is just a phase."

I showed her some vampire pictures. "What about her hair?"

"You had funny hair when you were a baby, too," Mom said.

"If Tootie isn't a vampire, then why are all of her favorite foods red—**BLOOD** red?"

"Because your baby sister has good taste," Mom cooed. "Don't you, Tootie-Wootie?"

Vampire Baby smiled.

"Would Tootie chew newspapers if she wasn't a vampire?" I asked Dad. "Perfectly normal," Dad answered.

"And dog toys? While the dog is chewing them?" Dad shrugged. "Nothing to worry about."

Nothing to worry about?

"YOUCH, TOOTIE! NO BITE!"

According to the books, vampires sleep during the day and stalk their prey at night. I set my alarm for midnight so I could catch Tootie in the act. Turns out I didn't need the alarm.

WAHHHH!

"If Tootie isn't a vampire, then why won't she sleep at night?"
I yelled.
"Your sister is not a vampire," Mom yelled back. "She's hungry.
And take off that garlic necklace!"

Since Mom and Dad wouldn't believe the truth about Tootie,
I was going to have to deal with Vampire Baby myself.
I waited for the perfect opportunity. It was shopping day,
and Mom had a long, long list.
"Don't worry—I'll take care of Tootie," I told her. "We'll be
in the costume section."

COSTUMES
AISLE 13

First I dressed Tootie in a Dracula cape and combed her hair.
Then I gave her the sign I'd made. "Here—hold this."

We were turning onto aisle 13 when I spotted them. Their collars were turned up, and their hair was slicked back, just like Tootie's.
"Look, Tootie, a vampire family! Exactly what I was hoping for. Now, smile and look cute."
Tootie smiled.

The vampire family smiled back.

"Look, Tootie—*fangs*, just like yours," I said.

Tootie waved her sign.

The vampire mother waved back. Her fingernails were blood red.

"Look, Tootie—red. This is your lucky day! A vampire baby like you belongs with a vampire family."

Tootie giggled.

"What an adorable baby," said the vampire father.

"What's your name?" The vampire mother asked, tousling Tootie's hair.

Tootie gurgled. I told them her name.

The boy vampire waggled his fingers as if he was playing the tickle game.

"Hello, cutie-wootie Tootie," he cooed.

Tootie smiled her extra-adorable baby smile.

"Want to come homey-womey with ussy-wussy?" he sang.

She gurgled and waved her chubby baby arms at him.

The boy vampire leaned in close, then closer . . .

"AAARGH!
YOW! OW! BAD BABY!"
he yelled, holding his nose.
"BAD, BAD BABY!"

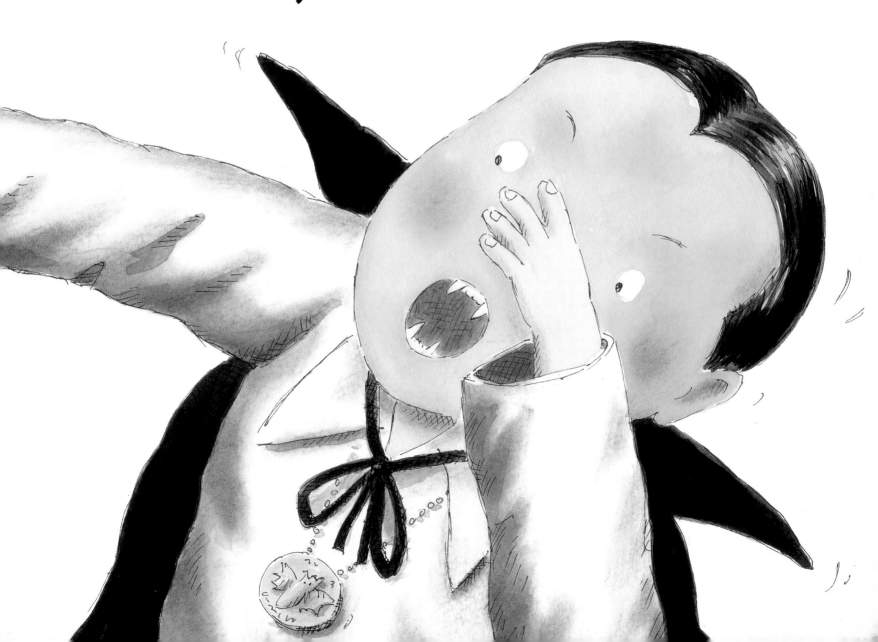

Tootie scrunched up her face and let out a squall.
"Back off, Bat Boy!" I said, scooping Tootie up.
"And watch how you talk to my little sister."

Tootie may be

a vampire baby.

But she's

my vampire baby.

CHOMP!

For Lori and Sarah, because you laughed first
K. B.

Text copyright © 2013 by Kelly Bennett
Illustrations copyright © 2013 by Paul Meisel

First edition 2013

Library of Congress Catalog Card Number 2012943658
ISBN 978-0-7636-4691-2

13 14 15 16 17 18 LEO 10 9 8 7 6 5 4 3 2 1

Printed in Heshan, Guangdong, China

This book was typeset in Kosmik.
The illustrations were done in acrylic, watercolor,
collage, pencil, ink, and pastel.

Candlewick Press
99 Dover Street
Somerville, Massachusetts 02144

visit us at www.candlewick.com